Clemens Finpol resides in Northern Wisconsin. He enjoys spending time outside and deer hunting in the fall. Currently working for a manufacturing company, his goal is to write many more novels for publishing and work from home someday.

I would like to dedicate this book to my loving family, for their immeasurable support has been nothing short of a motivator for writing this story. Additionally, I would like to thank Matthew Dietsche for igniting the voice inside of me, encouraging me to put my thoughts on paper, and for teaching me WHY to write. Last but not least, a large thank you goes out to our military men and women that are currently defending / have defended this great country. Your service is a sacrifice so that the rest of us can live free and pursue our dreams.

Clemens Finpol

PINK BISON

AUSTIN MACAULEY PUBLISHERS™

LONDON • CAMBRIDGE • NEW YORK • SHARJAH

Ordering Information
Quantity sales: Special discounts are available on quantity purchases by corporations, associations, and others. For details, contact the publisher at the address below.

Publisher's Cataloging-in-Publication data
Finpol, Clemens
Pink Bison

ISBN 9781647505585 (Paperback)
ISBN 9781647505578 (Hardback)
ISBN 9781647505592 (ePub e-book)

Library of Congress Control Number: 2021900915

www.austinmacauley.com/us

First Published 2022
Austin Macauley Publishers LLC
40 Wall Street, 33rd Floor, Suite 3302
New York, NY 10005
USA

mail-usa@austinmacauley.com
+1 (646) 5125767

I would like to thank Austin Macauley Publishers for giving me the opportunity to publish this piece and taking a chance on a young author.

Chapter 1

I awoke with a startle as my eyes flashed open to see a cigarette in the hands of my smoking companion. It was just Foley. His eyes were gazing over a field as he sat cross-legged on the cliff that we were perched on.

"Don't worry, I'm not going to kill ya," he said with a bit of a chuckle. That fucker was always giving me shit about being too cautious.

"I'd rather be aware of what's going on than dead," I replied with a sneer. It had to be about 5:30 in the morning. I had only gotten about three hours of sleep since my last turn to watch. I would say that it was about eighty degrees. The sun poked over the rocky mountaintops that stood there, marking the horizon. What a beautiful sight it was even though we were here to kill.

"Mayfield's gonna be coming out to our hole this morning," Foley mentioned. "I wouldn't be surprised if we started patrolling early today."

"Fuck. It never gets easier does it?"

"Hell no, man. If it were up to me, we'd camp out here all day and snipe any fucker that ambushed."

I laughed at that. Foley was one of the greatest guys that I had ever met. He was a strong man who had grown up on a farm back in Iowa. During training, he would always run next to me or sit by me at lunch and make the most crude and disgusting comments you could ever hear. However, he was a very smart fellow and knew how to survive out here.

"Got any more of that gum?" he asked.

"Yeah."

I pulled out a piece of *Pink Bison* and ripped it in half. He took the half and gave me a nod. I absolutely loved this gum. I had gotten it back home—

"WHAT WAS THAT?" Foley loudly whispered. "SHHH, I saw something move just down the hill!" Foley picked up his sniper rifle and examined the area through the scope. Despite his best efforts to give me crap, it seemed that HE was the one who was always being paranoid...

"Let me guess, it's a damn squirrel."

"SHUT THE FUCK UP!" I then peered out of the foxhole and noticed that there was a figure right down from the slope. It had to be from the movement that he had seen.

"I think I see—"

BANG. My ears rang as I sat scared in my boots and warm trench coat. I looked at Foley as he remained in his shooting position, not moving a single muscle. Five minutes went by before he looked at me.

"I think I got 'em."

We slowly made our way down the cliff. We were alert, but more so nervous. We finally reached the figure and realized that he had been alone. His uniform was covered in blood at the chest area. His ammunition belt had come detached from his torso and bullets were scattered across the ground. I shockingly glanced at Foley. He was staring down at the man. He looked sad, but I knew that he felt relieved that we were alive.

"Fucking cocksucker coulda blown our heads off!" he finally said.

Five minutes passed with us just standing there. I finally broke the silence with a "thanks bro."

Allan nodded. Allan was Foley's first name but you didn't call him that. Not because he would kill you if you did. You just didn't because he preferred Foley.

"WHAT THE HELL ARE YOU TWO DOING DOWN THERE?!"

We both knew that voice. General Mayfield stood at the top of the cliff near the foxhole with his hands up in the air.

"Be right up!" I replied.

*****

As we arrived back at the hole, Foley ejected the shell. Mayfield looked at him, confused.

"You shoot?"

"Yep."

"What?"

"A sniper. Down by that tree. Enough said."

Mayfield stared at him briefly and then nodded. "Alright, well, let's get going. The rest of the squad will be here shortly."

We started walking away from the hole. I looked back at the sun that had finally risen over the mountains.

Chapter 2

"Hey you two! Get anything?!"

Foley looked at me and shook his head. This question didn't surprise us as we suspected it to come from such a stupid fucker.

"He's going to get us killed someday," I said to Foley with a smile.

"Fucking-A Gus!" Mayfield snapped.

"Yeah," Foley finally replied as he ignored Mayfield's remark. "One."

"Oh. I'm sorry."

"Yeah, shut the hell up Atwood." A bunch of us laughed at this comment made by Haywood. The colonel let out a smile as he impatiently waited for further instruction.

"Well, the rest of the area seems clear," Mayfield said. "I guess we should start walking."

I took out a piece of gum. The bubble gum flavor quenched my desire for food. I blew a bubble as we began our patrol. We were supposedly going to hover on the edge of the mountains and scale around the hills that lay below them. As I moved to my position near the end, I looked at the black and white picture cutout of the girl Haywood had on the back of his helmet. She was pretty with wide eyes and brown hair, probably. Her smile was remarkable and she looked to be the happiest girl in the world. Though Haywood was married, he still figured that he had better have a hot chick on his helmet for good luck.

We walked for about an hour and a half. The hills were slippery as they shadowed the miraculously tall mountains. I noticed that the trees thinned out as we got farther away from the base of the mountains. Great for vision, but that went for the enemy too.

Mayfield put his hand up. Everyone stopped and glanced around the wooded area. We cautiously stood there for about five minutes. Sweat started to drip from my helmet as the temperature had noticeably risen ten to fifteen degrees since this morning. After Mayfield signaled to move on, I gathered my nerves and proceeded across the soft, brown terrain. I was second from the end with Foley standing to my left. To my right was Haywood, Mayfield, and Gus. Gus always complained about being on the end and said that I should be there because I was higher up in rank and had more experience. Those conversations didn't favor Atwood as they usually ended with a "go fuck yourself" from the general.

We were supposed to meet up with fifteenth by the end of our patrol. They were kind of our partner during these patrols. Only a few of them had gotten killed in the past few weeks and they had taken out many personnel throughout our mission. Also, they were pretty good guys who brought smiles to your faces during all of this turmoil.

The sun was hot and brighter than ever as we continued our journey through the forest. There was neither an animal nor insect out here. Just men who stealthily roamed through the bushes and shrubbery with cigarettes and guns. Boy was it quiet. I looked over at Haywood. Haywood was 39, so he was still pretty decent looking and had some hair left. The cigarette in his mouth wasn't lit as he was too nervous to stop and light it before we started our patrol. He looked at me and gave me a quick smile. This always brought some confidence to the mission within me knowing that he thought we were safe.

"GET DOWN!"

Machine gun fire had interrupted my thought process as I saw Stanley and everyone behind him hit the forest floor. I surveyed the thick woods as I dropped and lay on my stomach. My semiautomatic weapon was ready to go as I stood up and fired a few shots instinctively. However, Mayfield yelled at me to stay down and to crawl after him as he circled around the trees that stood in front of us. We all knew that the enemy probably couldn't see us but had fired when they had heard our footsteps. We laid down like sitting ducks in the thicket after regrouping. Shots fired and sent bullets hitting trees nearby and the ground next to the bush.

"GRANGER AND FOLEY FLANK LEFT! GUS AND STANLEY STAY WITH ME!" Mayfield ordered. Foley and I exchanged glances and bolted for an uprooted tree that provided cover about fifty feet away. *Fifteenth is gonna be fucked if they run into this.* Foley looked at me after we dove behind the tree. He nodded his head and provided cover fire while I took a quick peek over the mossy base of the tree. I saw the flash coming from guns about a hundred feet away. I ducked back down with Foley.

"HEY, I'LL COVER WHILE YOU SNEAK OVER TO THAT RIDGE AND TAKE 'EM OUT!" I yelled to him over the loud artillery.

"FUCK THAT! I AIN'T LEAVING YOU HERE ALONE!"

"I'LL BE FINE! I'LL GET SOME SUPPORT." I waved over to Gus, who was behind the thinnest tree you could find in that forest. He sprinted over and dove behind the tree as Foley made his way up the ridge. We probably fired a hundred rounds before Foley took his first shot. BANG! One of the guns seemed to have stopped firing in the distance. BANG! This time I saw the blood splatter from the head of one of the enemy soldiers. After this second shot, the other two retreated into the woods that sat behind them.

I looked upon the ridge at Foley. He sat in that same position, as if he was certain there were more.

"REGROUP!"

We all made our way back to the spot where Haywood and Mayfield were positioned.

"Damn! Scared the shit outta me!" Mayfield dropped his mag and put a full one in his rifle. "Atta boy Foley."

Foley's facial expression didn't change. He stood there with his blinking eyes and a mouth that couldn't decide if it wanted to smile or frown.

"Well, hopefully, them poor bastards from fifteenth won't be fucked," said Haywood.

Everyone exchanged looks as we loaded up and cautiously proceeded through the thick forest. After going through about twenty areas like this, it still wasn't easy to regain confidence after an attack. I took out another piece of gum and offered one to Foley. He nodded and took it. He seemed slightly more upbeat after he put it in his mouth.

Chapter 3

"You guys run into them, too?!" exclaimed one of the guys from fifteenth. "There were about fifteen of them running through when we had come through the edge of that woods. I think we got about four of them. They stopped and turned to shoot but I think they retreated when they saw our numbers."

Fifteenth had about twenty-five in their platoon. I don't know why some of them weren't assigned to transfer to our squad, but I figured that questioning it would upset some of them and interfere with our mission, so I kept my mouth shut.

"Yeah, Foley took out two of them with the o-six," Haywood replied. "Thick woods in there!"

"Damn straight. We came across a field and heard all of the gunfire. We were ready for 'em."

We settled down and started to eat whatever we had in our knapsacks. I pulled out a quarter of a sandwich and some saltines. My canteen was full of water. Warm, but still soothing. *It's gotta be a hundred and ten degrees out here.* Foley nudged me and offered his hand out with part of a chocolate bar in it. I gratefully accepted it with a smile and he gave me a thumbs up.

"Don't show this to any of the guys in fifteenth, or Mayfield," I murmured to him. He smiled and went on chewing his half of a banana.

"What the hell are we doing after this?" someone yelled amidst the lunch.

"Well, we are going to try and meet up with sixtieth," Haywood replied. He knew the General was the one who was supposed to be giving the orders, but figured he could chime in since he knew the plan. "They are coming from the northeast and we'll meet them at the camp."

This was music to my ears. I had been waiting for days for us to reach the camp. I had even questioned if it had ever existed. I finished my food and packed up. A pack of gum fell out of my bag and I quickly shoved it back in.

"Jesus Christ," Foley said. "How much of that do you have?"

"Enough," I joked with a smile. "Unless you go opening your big mouth about it!"

"Guess you'll have to give me more if you want me to shut up."

"Fucker."

With two groups moving closer toward the camp, I felt relieved of any stress or worry. I was right in the middle of the two platoons next to Foley. We were all spread out over a stretch of around a quarter of a mile. Mayfield was to my right. He looked surprised when he caught me smiling at him.

"We ain't safe yet."

That caught me a little off guard. I then focused on the fields ahead of me. We had about a mile to go before the camp would be reached.

"HEY! We just got word of some stragglers hanging around the area," yelled a captain in fifteenth.

"Must have been spotted from the camp," Foley said. "Might be the ones we ran into earlier."

I nodded at him, but while I was turning my head back to the field, I caught a glimpse of the bolt on his gun. In a delicate font were engraved two letters: *A.F.* It looked beautiful, as if the sun was hitting on it just right, as if it had been brand new out of the box, as if it had-

POW! POW! POW! Three men from fifteenth had shot at the field that sat off in the distance. I looked and saw a man running across the greenish hill into the woods. *Straggler fucker.*

"I got one!"

"Yeah, me too."

"I did, too. You see that one run into the woods?"

"Yeah."

I knew I had to quit getting distracted. Those men could have fired off a shot and hit any of us if those three hadn't been so alert. *Damnit Elliott, c'mon.*

"Let's proceed and radio in the other man we saw," Mayfield chimed in.

"Alright," the captain from fifteenth responded.

After about half an hour, we had made it to the camp. Sixtieth hadn't gotten there yet, so we all pulled up a seat on rocks, stumps, and the chairs that lay scattered across the ground. Our squad moved away from the others. Haywood started talking:

"Well, this day has been a huge fucking scary nightmare."

"No doubt, dumbass," Mayfield retorted. "Pretty startling when a figure is running across the field and you aren't ready."

"Yeah, I'm surprised Foley didn't take them out!" Gus added.

"Shut up Gus," Foley replied.

"Hey, I'm just saying that you're a good shot."

"Yeah, well, I appreciate the compliment but I don't want to talk about battle now. How about a story, or a joke? Anyone?"

"I got one," Gus quickly remarked. "How many lawyers does it take to change a light bulb?"

"Damnit Atwood you told us that one YESTERDAY!" Haywood snapped. "Fuck, let's just sit here and enjoy not being fired upon."

Just then, sixtieth arrived. With about thirty in their platoon, it appeared that four of them had been injured. Major Leroy Daviss was at the front of the group with his machine gun slung around his shoulder.

"Leroy!" everyone announced joyfully. Leroy was an honest man who had been in the hospital for about two weeks during training. Some retard made a horrible mistake during a grenade-throwing demonstration. The idiot threw it and hit the wall of a structure that caused it to bounce back fairly close to them. Leroy pulled the kid behind a bunker, but the force from the explosion had resulted in him to be thrown about twenty feet onto the ground. Not as serious of an injury as it could have been, but enough to cause hospitalization. Since his recovery, it seems that Leroy has made friends with everyone he meets during the war.

"Hey guys, what's up?"

"Not much, just ran into some stragglers. You?" I replied.

"Well, we got pinned down by some troops near a river. We had to make a break to get to the woods to flank them, but four of our guys got hit. Pretty damn scary. Not anything serious though."

"God Damn pecker heads."

"Yep. I'm glad to see you guys though. I heard that we have to gear up and go out to the canyons."

"No, c'mon." The canyons was the nickname for the place that the enemy had their camp set up at. Hard to get to and hilly as hell. It was the perfect spot. Air support never touched any of their bases out there because of the well-hidden and dangerous location.

"Ouch, knew it was coming," Haywood said. "Just us, fifteenth, and you guys?"

"Yeah, the other companies are trying to flank on the west and east sides to force them into the canyons. Then, we can capture them at the heart of this forsaken country."

"Sounds like they got the easy job," Mayfield added. "Not even sixty men going up against hundreds on the outer part and thousands further in?"

"Well, if we can take the outer half, the reinforcements will meet up with us and help us capture the center of it all."

"Still sounds ridiculous."

"Damnit Daviss, this visit was supposed to be reassuring," Foley said with a smile. Leroy and I laughed while Gus took out his canteen and drank as he curiously looked at some of his shells.

The nice part was the fact that we got to stay at the camp for the night. However, the soldiers that were spotted had everyone on high alert and ready for ambush at any time with watchdogs all over the camp boundaries. Foley and I were in the tent counting some dog tags and playing cards all afternoon. It was about five when we ate dinner. Graham crackers and cheese. *Yum.* I opened up another piece of *Pink Bison* afterward. I still remember when I had been notified that I was going to be called into duty. I went down to *Hal's Store* and bought every pack they had.

"You must really like this gum!" Hal exclaimed. Hal was the nicest store owner you could find around in an Indiana small-town. His prices were cheap and he always helped you out if you needed to pay him back at a later time.

"Yeah, well, I'm going overseas soon, so I wanted to take some with."

"Oh, man." Hal had tears running down his cheeks. I had come to see him almost every day for the last ten years, and I could see that this shocked him. "Well, I'm sorry son. God bless you. And thank you for all the happiness you have given me over the years. I will see you when you get back." Afterward, I hugged him. We must have held each other for about two minutes, both of us sniffling and scared.

"Be good, Hal. And thanks for the gum." I smiled.

"No, no, no, thank you, soldier," he said as he saluted me. "And remember, sometimes we can't control what happens in life, because it happens for a reason that will benefit us later."

I looked at the piece of paper that lay in my helmet that had those words on it, next to a picture of my mom and dad. I knew that this battle with a country we hated because we didn't agree with them about something had to be fought. I don't know why—I just know that there was nothing I could do about it. *No use complaining about it if you can't control it, I guess.* I put the gum in my mouth and dealt the cards to Foley for the next game.

Chapter 4

What the hell happened? Foley got hit! Get a medic! Cover me, I'm going up to meet with the squad. NO! STAY HERE AND HELP US! GOD DANGIT FOLEY STAY WITH US! Where's Granger? ELLIOTT! COME HERE! STAY LOW! WHAT'S GOING ON? IT'S FOLEY, HE WANTED YOU TO COME HERE! ELLIOTT... YEAH FOLEY? OH MY GOD YOU'RE HIT! DAMNIT GRANGER SHUT UP! Tell... tell my parents that I love them. And Lucy... Tell her to meet another man and to... have... a good... life...

I sat up from my cot with a startle. *Just a dream? Yeah, you're good man.* It had to be about midnight. I looked over at the bed where Foley lay. His chest was raising and lowering slowly, but heavily. The sweat on my forehead was now starting to roll down my face. I looked on the inside of my helmet and saw my parents hadn't moved. *Lucy? What was Foley talking about?* I then realized that Lucy wasn't in my helmet. I slowly got up and tiptoed over to where Foley's sniper rifle was leaning against the edge of his bed. Once again, the *A.F.* on his rifle bolt looked astonishing, even now when the only thing that could light it up was the lantern. I grabbed his helmet and walked back over to my bed. I sat and turned over the helmet as I reached for a lantern that lay close by. I took out a picture of Foley's parents. *What am I doing? He wouldn't be doing this to me.* I put the picture back and turned the helmet over. As I reached for the lantern, a small slip of paper fell out. A beautiful young lady with curly hair and the whitest teeth sat smiling on a bench. It was a black and white picture, but it brought out the joy and colors in you when you looked at it. I turned it over and read the writing on it:

Foley, I am going to miss you so much. The time we've spent together the last few months has been the very best of my life. I want you to know that I love you and hope you come home safe. I will be here waiting when you get back. And, by the way, make sure to keep that ice cream off your face! Love, Lucy.

I took a quick look at the picture again and put it back in the exact spot where I assumed it had been sitting, behind the picture of his parents. I then brought the helmet back to the other side of the room and set it on top of the barrel of the rifle where it had sat before. Thousands of memories of my parents and friends, Lucy and Hal surfaced as I lay back down on my cot. My eyes grew heavy as I started to drift off to sleep. Haywood began coughing as I wandered into another unanticipated nightmare…

Chapter 5

I woke up around six o'clock. Foley had been out of bed and so had Haywood. Mayfield was outside the tent when I opened the flap.

"Go get Atwood up before I shoot his ass," Mayfield ordered with a smirk. I obliged and shook Gus as he rolled around with a moan. He looked mad, but I knew he had gotten enough rest, considering he had hit the hay early.

"Gus, Mayfield said if you don't get up, he'll cut your fucking nuts off."

"SHIT!" Gus exclaimed as he shot up from his pillow. He then tried to tackle me as I backed up laughing. "You son of a gun, Elliott!"

"Let's get something to eat, you idiot."

We walked over to where a fire lay burning underneath.

"Egg you two?"

"Yessir."

"Yeah."

I watched as Leroy let the egg sizzle for another moment or two and then slide it onto a plate. It looked weird, but smelt amazing as I took a bite. Gus ate his in about five seconds then grabbed his canteen for a swig. Then he lit a cigarette and looked up at the sun.

"A hundred yet?"

"Probably," Leroy replied. "And will probably get to about a hundred and twenty by this afternoon."

"Damn."

Mayfield walked over to where we were sitting.

"We leave in a half, boys. Eat well and gear up. Going to be the worst day of the mission."

Everyone looked at each other after those comments. Leroy tried to remain confident as he continued to break out a smile here and there, but we all knew it was going to be a horrible day and that everyone was scared out of their minds. But did it really matter what day it was? Every day was hell.

Haywood walked over with a canteen in one hand and his gun in the other. He sat down next to Gus and me as we gave him nods.

"Well, I guess today is the day we decide if we believe in God or not, eh?" he remarked.

"Keep it to yourself, Haywood!" Leroy countered with a scowl. "How about we shut up and enjoy the time we have left before we walk into hell."

"Agreed," I commented while my stomach dropped. Whenever Leroy was scared, you knew it was going to be a heck of a day.

*****

"HEY! SHUT UP!"

We all halted after Mayfield's warning. The dangerously thick, green forest was the worst place we could have been right now. With about fifty-eight men, we knew an ambush could be handled fairly well, but could also spell trouble if bullets were sprayed. Water dripped off the leaves of the trees in the wet area as the sun poked through the ceiling of the umbrella-like treetops.

"TWO!" Mayfield whispered. We all looked up across a small marsh and saw two men smoking with their rifles held loosely in front of their crossed legs.

"FOLEY AND GRANGER GO AROUND AND SET UP ON THE LEFT! LOOK FOR A HIGH SPOT, A RIDGE OR SOMETHING! THE REST OF US WILL GO SEE IF THERE ARE MORE, A CAMP MAYBE OR SOMETHING. WE WILL SIGNAL IF IT IS JUST THOSE TWO TO TAKE THEM OUT. SILENCER FOLEY?"

"YEAH."

"GOOD LUCK, GENTLEMEN. WE WILL SEE YOU SHORTLY."

Foley gave me a nod as we then flanked up to the left of the marsh. We quietly climbed a hill that was about twenty feet shorter than the ridge where the men sat. We crawled behind the thick trees. *What a horrible place those men are in! Out of all of this thick forest…*

Foley nudged me and motioned his head toward a nice-looking hill with shrubbery and thick tree trunks. I nodded and followed him closely and we lied on our stomachs as we saw the men stand up and stretch. We were about seventy yards away. Foley looked through his scope as I looked over to where Mayfield had supposedly led the men to. The radio finally came on:

Looks clear. Take the shots. We will take the other one out if you don't have a second shot.

"Gum?"

I looked at Foley with confusion. He gave me a nod as I handed him a piece of *Pink Bison*. Only Foley would be worried about gum during a situation like this.

"Thanks."

I nodded as he took his position. I held up my gun, ready to fire if there were suddenly more soldiers around. I had a thirty-shot clip in my machine gun and a ten shot semiautomatic rifle on my bag. I quickly switched to the semi-auto after realizing it was more ideal.

We could barely see the men, but I knew Foley had a shot. I could hear his teeth chomping on the bubble gum…

BANG! One man rolled down the hill uncontrollably. BANG! I saw the other man fall backward. Two clean hits.

"Confirmed," I radioed back to Mayfield.

"Why'd you shoot?!"

I looked at the rifle in front of me. Both Foley and I watched the smoke rise from the muzzle of my gun. A confused look was planted on both of our faces. I never noticed I had pulled the trigger on my weapon. Hell, I didn't even know I was aiming at the man. I tried to suppress the thought of taking another human life that was knocking at the wall of my mind. I always did after I had done so. "I'm sorry."

"Hell of a good shot man," Foley reassured. "No more enemy around. I think we are fine."

We carefully made our way back down the hill and walked back over to where Mayfield had the rest of the men.

"WHAT THE FUCK?! FOLEY, I SAID SILENCER! I DIDN'T HEAR THE FIRST ONE-"

"I shot sir," I hesitantly chimed in.

"WHAT?!"

"HEY, FUCK OFF MAYFIELD. MAN'S DEAD RIGHT? JESUS CHRIST, HE FIRED ON INSTINCT. HELL OF A GOOD SHOT, TOO."

Everyone was surprised by this outburst from Foley. Mayfield started at him then signaled to us to start walking again. I nodded to Foley as he smiled at me. Leroy gave me a thumbs up for reassurance and Gus looked like he had just wet his pants. We walked around the marsh and finally came to a more visual-friendly area. The fields interrupted the tall and thick trees which outlined the vast and prairie-like landscape.

Chapter 6

We patrolled for hours. It was hot and dry. Everyone was cautious as we approached the woods that were sitting before the foot of the mountains where the canyons were located.

The fields didn't offer much resistance. Men must have been scattered around the edges where the other companies had tried to flank. Heavy gunfire in the distance made us all question the status of our fellow soldiers. But when the other platoons had radioed in only minimal resistance and few casualties, we felt reassured. However, everyone knew this meant the worst combat was yet to come.

"What time do you think it is?" Gus finally asked, breaking the silence that loomed for hours.

"It's about two-thirty, Atwood," Mayfield responded.

"Damn."

I took out a piece of gum and handed it to Gus. He looked happy and appreciative as he popped it into his mouth and munched away. I looked at my rifle. It had sat in my hands for about four hours straight now. I didn't mind, however, since it provided me with a sense of relief in case of an attack.

I looked down the line of tired, sweaty soldiers. They looked focused, yet annoyed. Leroy was close to the end. We were fairly close together; I'd say within a quarter-mile. You could see the mosquitos and other small bugs buzzing furiously around each individuals' face. Although there hadn't been many bugs the past few days, the onslaught of them now made up for the paradise we had before. Nobody was remotely thinking of putting their arms in the air to swat the demons though.

*****

I rushed behind a bush when the attack came. We had just made our way into another wooded area filled with ravines and rolling hills. Gunfire had taken out two of our men already and it seemed that we were pinned down.

"GRENADES!"

I pulled the pin and let one go. It was hard to find the time to throw one let alone pull your gun up to take a shot. I barely saw the explosion behind the flashes and smoke that filled the air in front of my face. Gus and I had been next to each other ever since Mayfield tried to fire back at them, but we were noticeably outnumbered. This area was only the beginning of the destruction that lay ahead, IF we were able to make it that far.

It was about fifteen minutes before they started rushing up to our barriers, which were fallen trees and rock piles. Gus and I alone had taken out about twelve men that were trying to dive into our faces to stab us. Foley was somewhere off to the left firing every once in a while. That's when you'd see a head explode. When Foley shot.

Haywood was on the thirty cal. trying to assist us in taking out the ones who were rushing at our line. Mayfield was now giving orders that nobody could hear nor understand. He would stand up and then duck back down when he realized he was an idiot for even showing his face.

"REQUEST FOR AIR SUPPORT ON SECTOR ONE! I REPEAT, AIR SUPPORT ON SECTOR ONE!"

The call was answered and about ten seconds later, we saw the enemy disappear as we retreated back into the thicker shrubbery for cover.

"LET'S GO!"

Foley came running over. It seemed that he didn't give a damn about where Mayfield wanted him. Mayfield didn't say anything though because he knew that Foley was a vital part of our group and that he had saved his ass numerous times in situations like this one. He gave me a pat on the shoulder and Gus a smile as I put a new clip in and continued cautiously through the forest.

*****

"You wanna sleep?"

"I can watch."

"You sure?"

"Yeah."

I took my position at the edge of the foxhole as Foley did the best he could to make himself comfortable. He had given me some of his banana earlier for dinner as we had to do the best we could to eat and stay alert. I took out some more *Pink Bison* and perched my gun on the edge of the hole. I was nervous, yet relieved that we hadn't seen a soldier in four hours, even though we had only moved a mile during that whole time period. Gus had everyone laughing when he had hit the deck after hearing the sound of bombs being dropped miles away. Haywood had been smoking while we were pinned down surveying the treetops for snipers. This made me laugh afterward, even though the situation wasn't really that funny. I got one that had poked his arm out from a branch he was sitting on and Foley hit one right in the guts as he fell with a loud thud. Nobody had ever seen the fucker way off in the distance and were surprised when they heard the shot and turned to see Foley sitting in his shooting stance with one knee up, ready to send another one to the grave. Zero attacks throughout the rest of the evening provided some sense of comfort for all of us.

"Here, you should have my gun." I looked and Foley had his hand out holding the sniper rifle as he lay there with his eyes closed. I took it and looked through the scope. The land below was beautiful with tops of trees covering the ground that was questioned to exist. We were on a huge cliff again, and I felt relieved having the large number of men looking off in the distance next to me. Though half of them were sleeping, it was still calming. I thought back to the night before, when I had read the note from Lucy.

"Hey, Foley?"

"Yeah."

"I have to tell you something. I know you've been pretty honest with me as I have been with you, but last night, I got a little curious and saw the picture of Lucy. I was wondering why you had never told me about her."

"Oh, that." There was a long pause and I thought that Foley had fallen asleep. But I glanced at him to see that his eyes were staring at the brown ground next to him.

"I'm sorry, man. I'll mind my own business."

"Nah, no biggie man. I will tell you about her. But not tonight. I am tired."

"Goodnight man."

"Yeah. Don't let any bastards kill me in the next four hours."

"I thought it was three-hour shifts?"

"It was until you went snooping." He chuckled.

"Damnit. You got me there."

Chapter 7

"Fuck."

I had heard this. Even though the whisper shouldn't have penetrated my deep sleep, it had. Foley had his gun ready in the dark, moonlit night that provided so much illumination you'd think the war gods were on our side.

"What's up?"

"We got about fifty infantrymen patrolling down there."

"What's going on?" Mayfield had heard the commotion and came crawling over.

"Look."

Mayfield joined us in gazing at the enemy. They were loose, unaware, relaxed. They didn't know that we were all the way up here and had the high ground. Hell, they probably thought we were all dead.

"Well, we could try and wait them out to see if they go around these cliffs," Mayfield said. "Or, we take most of them out and risk them knowing our position."

"Damnit." Haywood had now made his way over to where we were positioned. Gus was still sleeping, somehow. All the other men were up and alert, wondering what the fuck we were going to do.

"Ouch," Leroy whispered loudly from further on down the line. "Yo, Mayfield, what is the plan?"

For the first time during the whole mission, General Douglas Mayfield looked unsure of what to do. After about twenty seconds of our eyes glaring at his, he finally responded. "WE WAIT."

I took out my rifle and slowly crawled to the edge of the hole. I quietly pulled the action back and let the pin go. I was ready. I was mad. I was going to kill someone who wouldn't let me sleep. I took out a piece of gum and handed it to Foley. He ripped it in half and gave me the other part. He nodded and we both aimed at the men below. Gus came weaving his way over and lay next to us with his machine gun. Foley shook his head as Gus shrugged and smirked, which was followed by a yawn.

We watched the men for about two hours, observing their every move as we scaled the edges of the cliffs in order to confirm they were avoiding the climb up to where we were positioned.

"We should take them," Foley kept saying to Mayfield. "What if they come and hit our men from the backside?"

"Other companies have been alerted," Mayfield confidently replied. "They will be ready for them. Hell, they may wander so far out that by the time they return, the canyons will be ours."

"So, we are risking their lives so that we can be safe for a little while? That's not what soldiers do!"

"Those are your orders, Allan."

Foley knew that he had been shut down. Even Mayfield never called him Allan. He meant business now, and Foley shut up after that remark.

Eventually, the infantry passed and we were able to go back to resting. However, we moved half of our men to the rear of the camping area, just in case an attack was to arise from there. I went back to sleep and didn't wake up until morning, surprised.

"Why didn't you wake me, man?" I asked Foley. Foley was still perched on the edge looking through his scope.

"I felt that I should be ready, man. You look tired. No biggie."

"Wow. Thanks. But I feel bad man."

"Give me some more gum and we will call it good."

This time, I whipped out a whole pack. Foley took one piece out and tried to give the rest back, but I refused it with a wave of my hand. He nodded and stored it away in his pack.

"Well, it looks alright. We have to keep moving." Mayfield had put his hands on our shoulders and calmly told us the situation. He seemed relieved, yet looked somewhat guilty when we turned around to give him a nod.

"Hey, sir, sorry about last night." Foley had stood up with a hand out.

"Soldier, there is no need to apologize for looking out for your companions." Mayfield shook his hand and looked at me afterward. "Could I have a piece of that gum?"

"Yessir." He took it and chuckled.

We geared up and started our way back down toward the forest floor that housed the enemy who would be at our throats for the rest of the afternoon.

*****

"Don't move."

"Help me, God."

"Be quiet…"

We were fucked. After we had made our way down the cliffs, our ears were ringing with mortar fire that had been launched from who the hell knows where. After ten men were killed, it seemed that we were done for. However, Mayfield lifted our spirits with some quick words of encouragement. If I recall correctly, it was something like "LET'S KILL THESE FUCKS!" and "THIS IS OUR WAR!" We then proceeded to make a dent in their numbers with me and Haywood breaking out the thirty cal. again and Foley moving up to a tree to give us some relief.

And now, after firing was halted and we were told to get down and stay down, more troops were on their way and once again, we were to remain in our position. I think we planned to wait until they got close and then ambush. But with about forty men, we knew it wouldn't work.

"Don't worry, we'll get out of this." Mayfield was angry and ready to kill.

"General, we gotta retreat and regroup. Maybe we can flank later?!" Foley was questioning him again, but Mayfield knew Foley was right.

"What do you guys think?"

"I DON'T WANNA GET STEPPED ON AND STABBED!" Gus exclaimed.

"Alright, sorry, I got caught up in the fight. Let's go boys."

Just then, we heard gunfire from the north. It wasn't the enemy though, as we looked up and saw them approaching. They turned and returned fire, but were too late as bullets knocked off helmets and pierced soldier bodies. We looked and saw the sixty-second infantry coming through with about forty more men. We grouped up with them, now firing profusely at the bodies that were surrounded ahead. Shouts of joy and anger filled the air as we were able to take out all of them, probably about sixty men.

*****

"Damn. I almost got us killed," Mayfield mentioned afterward. We were sitting on a riverbank, getting ready to cross. He was almost in tears.

"You can't let the anger and ferocity of war get in the way of making decisions," Haywood advised. "Luckily, your plan to stay where we were actually worked." He smiled. I was surprised how supportively Haywood spoke to Mayfield.

"Yeah, don't do that again," one of the men from sixty-second had interrupted our conversation. "You're a good general, lead this courageous group of men with confidence, not with a grudge."

"Yeah. C'mon boys, let's cross this fucking river," Mayfield ordered with a laugh afterward.

"Hey, where's Foley?" I asked.

"He is eating somewhere, I think," Mayfield replied.

I wandered over to a riverbank behind a group of trees. Foley was sitting there, crying. I looked over his shoulder quietly and saw the picture of Lucy in his hand.

He turned his head and slowly turned it away again.

"I almost lost her today. I'm scared," Foley wept.

I put my arm around his shoulder and pulled out a piece of gum. This one had an actual picture of the logo *Pink Bison* had used back in the days that it first came out. Foley smiled and wiped his tears away. He then took it and put it in his bag. He looked at the picture of Lucy and said, "You know Granger, Lucy and I wanted to get married, but then I got called into battle. I told her that we could do it before I left but she refused… You see I had met her…"

"Not now man, we gotta go."

"C'mon man, just a minute."

"Alright."

"You see, me and her had met at a bar in Iowa when I was nineteen. I walked over to her and introduced myself. She looked happy and eager to get to know me, so we went to the edge of a lake afterward. We were talking… and flirting… and things got pretty serious in just those few hours. Our connection was so… perfect. We spent about eight years together. Then I got called in.

"A couple of nights before I left, we went to this ice cream shop and we were sitting next to each other in a booth. Her white dress was short enough to where her legs looked so elegant, but don't worry, it was appropriate." Foley and I laughed. "I asked her to marry me the next day, but she said that we should wait until after I got back. I had brought up the scenario that I may not return, and she started crying. I pulled her in and the cone in her hand smashed into my face. I stared at her as she slowly started giggling. She then said '*make sure you don't have ice cream on your face overseas.*'" Foley sniffed back a few tears. "Everything was just fine afterward and I left a few days later. When we said goodbye, she didn't cry. She had a huge smile on her face. She was so strong…holding back tears so I wouldn't feel so bad. I can't wait to marry her…"

"Wow," I said. "Foley, you will marry Lucy. You will get home. And we will win this war."

"Yeah," he replied. "Thanks, Granger."

"No problem, man."

"Let's go."

"Yeah, let's go and kill some more of these cock bites."

Foley laughed and wiped the rest of his tears away as we grabbed our gear and walked to where the rest of the group was.

Chapter 8

Our company continued to move forward. It was us, fifteenth, sixtieth, and sixty-second that were marching right down the throats of the enemy. With about eighty soldiers total to begin with, we were down to about fifty-five throughout the four platoons. However, twenty-five deaths resulting from all the attacks, ambushes, and fearful nights that we fought through was pretty good in my opinion.

We were climbing some hills that would lead us right to the foot of the canyon "headquarters." It was dusk, with the heavier darkness clouding our vision every next minute. We had to make it to the top of the hill in order to gain the high ground because we knew that we had to be on high alert throughout the entire night.

"We got about two hundred more yards men, then we can rest," Mayfield whispered.

"Damnit," Gus replied.

Just then, a faint sound got everyone's attention. We all stopped and looked up. It sounded like a whirring and rumbling sound that kept getting louder and louder. All of a sudden, my stomach dropped. Everyone knew what it was. Plane engines.

"COVER!" Mayfield roared as the plane's engines neared with a loud whistle.

We all found some uprooted trees as we dove right into the roots of them. Me, Gus, and Foley were all huddled together as we saw dirt explode from the ground around us. I looked over at Mayfield and Haywood. They were both freaking out, trying to give orders over the loud explosions from the bombs that dropped overhead. I turned my head as Foley grabbed my shoulder and pointed to the two dead men that lay in the middle of the ruckus. We both figured we were fucked as we watched the bombs continue to hit the ground around us.

*****

"DAMNIT! DAMNIT! WHAT THE HELL WAS THAT?!"

Haywood was on the radio trying to contact dispatch. As red as his face was, he seemed more scared than angry. I was lying next to Foley, not moving a muscle, not even breathing. I finally took out a piece of gum and slowly put it in my mouth. Foley tapped my shoulder and I handed him a piece of gum. He barely moved while taking it.

"Sixtieth company, do you copy, I repeat, do you copy?"

"THERE ISN'T ANY RADIO OP FOR SIXTIETH, THEY BLEW HIS FUCKING HEAD OFF!" Haywood stormed. "WHERE THE HELL WAS THE WARNING ON THAT ONE, HUH?!"

"I am sorry to tell you that those weren't enemy bombs…there was a mix-up on the locations…we told them

sector three and they hit sector four…in our defense, we didn't know you guys were that close to the canyons…won't happen again… over and out."

Haywood sat there with the phone in one hand and his mouth wide open. He, like all of us, couldn't believe what was just said.

"So…that's what happening," Haywood finally began saying slowly. "We are going to die. Not because there is an ENEMY FIRING AT US, but because OUR OWN FUCKING SIDE IS RETARDED?!"

Nobody said a word as Haywood lay down and started to weep slightly. Mayfield went over to his side and, after a few minutes, finally spoke:

"Well, I guess we should hunker down here and be on alert in case the enemy heard all that shit and is on their way. Goodnight boys, make sure every other one is on watch."

"Hey." Foley poked me.

"Sup?"

"I'll watch first."

"You sure?"

"Yeah."

"Okay, thanks. Hey man… I'm sure nothing like that would happen again…"

"Yeah, let's hope."

"Wake me in three."

"Yep."

Chapter 9

Elliott, you're making me all hot! That's my mission young lady. Gosh, you're so damn beautiful. Let me show you how hot you are—NO! Not here! Awww, come on there, Monica. I'll be leaving in only a month! Well…okay. Help me with my dress—

PING. It was the same sound that a bullet makes when it hits a rock. I awoke to this. *FUCK.* I was more upset about the recalled memory that had turned into my dream being ruined by someone's stray fucking bullet.

I glanced over to where Foley should have been. Gone. I turned to several other positions that surrounded mine. Nope, not at any of those either. I had my back turned to the north when all of a sudden, the sound of a knapsack and heavy boots thundered in from behind me.

"Holy shit Foley!" I murmured as he had come in from behind me like a dart.

"Easy there, Granger." Foley didn't smile when he said this. There was a mix of a surprised and startled expression as he peered over the uprooted tree in front of us.

"Where the fuck did you go?"

"Mayfield and I were on watch at around two when these two objects were moving to the right of us. He gave me a nod and I went to the north to check it out. Half-tracks. Each of them with one person atop the hatch. I got into position and took a shot at the first one. I hit that fucker. The second one missed. Somehow that God damn lucky fuck knew where the shot came from and fired back at me. He hit about three feet over my head. Must have been a semi-auto. The next shot from me missed and hit the half-track."

That's where I heard that.

"I was then smart enough to use the silencer and let her fly on the second one. I was embracing for another shot, but the machines just kept moving to the southwest. I'm guessing they saw our group and wanted to pass by without too much flak. I guess it was worth losing two fucks. Now I'm even more worried."

By now, everybody had woken up and was on high alert. There was a rumor going around that Foley was nearing his seventieth confirmed. I didn't want to ask him about it because he didn't care.

"Well, I think that we are sitting ducks here now," Mayfield said upsettingly as he squirmed over to where we were. "Better get a move on."

It was three o'clock now. *Fuck.* I wanted Monica back in my mind for just a second, but couldn't focus on the vixen now. We had more work to do...

"Another nightmare, Elliott?" Foley had helped me up from my knees.

"I guess so man. It's weird how we have more of those when we're awake than when we are asleep."

"For fucks sake, I thought I was the only one who figured that out."

Another stick of *Pink Bison* came out of his backpack. He offered me half and insisted that I take it when I initially refused. A nod and then a turn to the south followed. *Another uphill stroll.* I was starting to think God was just messing with us now. Out of the corner of my eye, I noticed Gus pulling up his pants near his downed tree. A shit, knowing him.

*****

We only walked for about thirty minutes. It was exceptionally quiet—an eerie type of quiet—an unfortunate one where you know something is about to happen…

SHOOP. I had barely heard it. It was an odd but uncanny noise. *Bullet.* That thought lasted for half a second when I heard the THUD. Everyone fired their necks around to see Leroy on the ground with blood gushing from his chest and the sound of him choking up what was left of his breath. Immediately, Gus and Haywood started firing their machine guns in the general direction from which the bullet had come from to pierce Daviss's body. Foley and I crouched next to him in disbelief, taking demands from the medic and trying to follow instructions as best we could in the traumatic moment.

"STAY WITH ME!" the medic roared into the unresponsive face that lay underneath his torso.

Leroy's eyes started to halfway roll into the back of his head. *It's over.* I continued to push on the pressured area as gauze and bandages flooded the chest cavity. We all knew.

A few seconds later, there was no movement and the medic had thrown down the materials in disgust next to the still figure that lay in front of us.

"I'm sorry boys." The medic gave a sorrowful look to all of us as we all sat there with empty expressions on our faces. Nobody had returned fire during the tragic event, so we knew there was a loose sniper amongst the wilderness.

"Well," Foley finally broke the silence, "looks like we have a new task at hand. Granger, you gonna be my right-hand man while we take that motherfucker out?"

"Hell yes, he is," chimed in Mayfield. "You two go on ahead on the right and we'll continue up the middle. Chances are, he'll expect us to break course, but maybe we can get him to poke out if we continue on our current path."

"Sounds good to me," I finally added. I popped in two more pieces of *Pink Bison* this time. Man, this was getting stressful.

Foley and I were about fifty to sixty yards west of our comrades. Fifty-two people in the middle and two on the right....*stupid on paper, but necessary*. We had all disregarded the thoughts of vengeance and justice because we knew that those were the reasons for this formation. Nobody wanted to admit it though.

I had my semi-auto ready with ten rounds in the clip and Foley had his .30-06 ready at the shoulder. We had walked about a quarter of a mile. Who knew where the fuck this guy was or if he was even alive anymore. Foley jabbed me with the butt of his rifle.

"Leroy was a great guy," he whispered. "I had gotten to know him very well these past two months. I guess he had a dad that survived cancer. He was going to retire and take him fishing in Alaska as a welcome home present. Too bad."

I hesitated before I spoke. "Yeah, man…he seemed to be a go-to. He's in God's hands now." Just then, Foley's arm swung out like a turnstile ready to halt the next individual in a subway tunnel.

"Look."

On a small ridge sat a man eating a sandwich in a tan-colored uniform, if you wanted to call it that. In his lap was a scoped rifle. He had his clip on the ground next to him, and it looked as if he thought there was nobody in the jungle but him.

Foley discretely signaled over to Mayfield, receiving a nod in return. I nodded then when he wagged two fingers and pointed to a small ridge near our position. The rest of the company knelt down and waited. *Looks like it's time for the two rascals to go to work.*

I crept up the ridge next to Foley, keeping an eye on the man the entire time. We reached the ridge in what felt like half an hour. I lay prone as Foley got down on two knees. He then lifted one up to sit ninety degrees to the earth. His classic shooting position. I grabbed my binoculars and looked below.

"About ninety yards I'd say," I whispered to Foley.

"I agree."

"Are you ready?"

"Yep. Let me know when this wind dies down." Foley finished screwing on the suppressor.

I hadn't even noticed the wind. I then waited as the slight breeze went extinct.

"Okay, man, go ahead."

BANG. It was another slow-motion moment that I was getting so sick of experiencing. I watched as the bullet severed the neck of the individual below, an immediate decapitation and kill.

"Tango down," I told Foley.

BANG. My ears rang on this one. *Another shot? Where was the other fucker?* I hadn't noticed anyone else around. I then quickly shouldered my gun, thinking that we might have accidentally become surrounded during the midst of our revenge-driven mission.

"Another through the chest for good measure, eh?" Foley looked at me with a smirk as I felt a very small smile come across my face. I looked back down through the binoculars and noticed that there wasn't much left of the same man's chest cavity.

"Yeah, Leroy was worth two."

"My thoughts exactly Granger. Where's that gum?"

I pulled out a piece and gave it to him. We then walked over to the group of people who lay cautiously next to a large group of bushes.

"Good work, men. Let's go. We're about halfway up the canyons."

The fifty-four of us walked into the tree-covered landscape, and into the unknown that was yet to haunt us.

Chapter 10

Of course, nobody wanted to be in this situation, but the fact that we couldn't even get a God damn tank in here just made it worse. I'd say we were about three-fourths of the way up through the canyons. You couldn't really tell due to the land leveling off every time you reached the top of an incline, but we kinda knew where the hell we were.

We heard the flak from a ways away. We knew that we were in for another standoff. Unfortunately, we had limited numbers and supplies. A few guys from sixty-second carried mortars. Only one bazooka and about ten 30-caliber machine guns made up the rest of our bigger artillery. As we took cover in thick undergrowth, a few of us were able to find large dirt banks to duck behind. *Must have been left here from a prior encounter…*Heavy fire hit the barrier, but we knew we'd be all right for a little bit. Haywood discovered there were three machine guns sitting in man-made towers about seven feet off the ground. They were all covered in shrubs and leaves, so it was only visible by the flash coming from the ends of the barrels.

"Foley!" yelled Mayfield over the loud racketing of rounds demolishing our wall. "Take Granger and flank right! Sixtieth and sixty-second will stay here and try to drop some shit on top of them. The rest of us and fifteenth will spread out and provide suppressing fire!"

Before he was even done talking, Allan and I had sprinted along the edge of the bank and dove behind a group of downed trees. We skirted up a small hill as we watched the lead smash into and above our comrades below. There was always at least one of the guns firing away. It was curious that this was all their assault had. *Something isn't right, either there's more coming or they're planning an attack from the left flank. But wait, there's kind of a ridge there…so that wouldn't work. No wonder Mayfield made us go right…*

Foley and I reached the flat spot on the hill and made sure that forces weren't taking us by surprise around us.

"Looks good," said Foley. He quickly chambered a round and lay prone as the noise continued below. "I have a shot at two of them."

"Okay man, I'll keep watch from up here and let you know if we gotta get the fuck out of here-"

FWOOP! The sound was the scariest I had ever heard. I felt my stomach drop to the ground as a large, deeply colored red hole had formed on my shin followed by a surge of pain that almost made me leap down the hill.

"FUCK!" Man, the thing hurt. I rolled over and scooted about twenty feet away from where I lay before, just down the side of the hill. I looked over and saw the medic scampering across the line of machine guns that fired in front of him. A large shadow came over me as Foley leaped down to my side.

"Whoa Granger! He got ya good."

"Bastard. Did you radio for the medic?" Even getting words out of my mouth was getting more difficult. *Fucking cocksucker.*

"Yeah, quick aren't I?" Foley's jokes weren't followed by a smile from him, as he seemed very concerned with my wound.

"All right guys," the medic said as he knelt by my side. "Nothing dramatic here, gonna hurt like a fucker for a sec though…" The medic ripped out a few bandages and sprinkled on some powder shit before adding some liquid into the gash. It didn't hurt too much more but then Foley told me to turn my head and look down at our guys for a second.

"MOTHER OF CHRIST!" I shrilled. "HOLY GOD! AHH, AHH, OWW!"

I wasn't shocked by what the hell was going on down below. The asshole had shoved a blade in my leg and peeled out a small oval figure.

"There's your trophy," the medic said as he handed it to me and finished his job.

"Wow, didn't know you'd take it out," Foley said. He looked like he was gonna pass out.

"Don't faint on me you fucker, you've got four people to kill now," I jabbed at Foley.

"Oh yeah, the bad news. That little buddy came from our sniper friend we met earlier."

"HUH?!" My surprised reply came out as the medic slid back down the hill to go assist a guy on the far edge of our firing line.

"Yeah, I saw him in that middle bunker. I noticed a different flash right as you yelled out. I threw a few back down there to shut him up for a second and then came to help you."

"I thought we killed that fucker!" Now it looked like the machine-gun fire was slowing down just a hair. Not much, but you start to notice this shit after being in hell for so long.

"I did too, but that S.O.B. we nailed before could have been anyone. Anyways, I'm not sure, but for our sake, we'd better treat it as so."

I nodded as I crawled prone up the side of the hill back to the top. *This is going to be a fucker to walk on.* Foley was by my side as we stopped, barely peering over the edge of the peak.

"Here." Foley handed me his jewel.

"I'm not holding your fucking rifle."

"Nope, you're shooting. You can't run, so I'll take your semi and run down the side. When he pops out to cook my goose, knock his head off. It's only fair."

"WHAT?!" It sounded like I was yelling louder than the flak below. "FUCK THAT! I've only shot a longer distance in basic!"

"PUT THE FUCKING CROSSHAIRS ON THE HEAD AND PULL THE TRIGGER! It's only like eighty yards man. I'm going, shut the fuck up."

Foley grabbed my rifle that lay next to me and knelt, ready to spree.

"Okay man, don't let him kill me."

I wanted to talk about this for a sec more but was too late as he ran down the side of the hill. He was about fifty yards south of the crossfire, and was gonna run somewhat parallel to it once he hit the bottom, I assumed.

I had the rifle resting on the peak of the hill on a small log, about four inches in diameter. I kept the scope on the middle bunker, but made sure I could see the other two in case the asshole had moved. Foley jutted left and right down the steep hillside as I waited patiently. A small figure peered through the hole in the bunker. It looked like a stick, but I knew it was a barrel. The only reason I could see it was because the bunker was angled somewhat away from our position, so we couldn't see the men in there super well. But the figure that came from the side was obvious enough to me to where I knew it was my target. I could have taken out three of these gunners by now, but knew that would give away my position and strike a nerve with Foley. This sniper needed to go.

My finger sat on the front of the trigger. I still couldn't quite see the figure holding the weapon. *Foley needs to dodge at least one.*

BANG. It was nearly simultaneous. As I saw the flash come out of the barrel, I fired right above it. I saw what looked like a man being swung off his feet as blood sprayed out of the hole. I also noticed that the machine gun had quit firing too. *Did I hit the wrong fucker?!*

BANG… BANG. Those thoughts quickly left my head as I instinctively fired at the other gunners. The same result with these machine guns. No more fire. I sat on the scope for what felt like five minutes, gazing down toward that middle bunker, waiting for the fucker to fire again. I almost sprang out of my gear when I felt a huge smack on my back plant me on the ground.

"Good shooting my man!" yelled Mayfield. *When the fuck was this guy in this good of a mood?* He had come with the rest of the folks up the side when firing had ceased momentarily.

"Yeah, any word from Foley?"

"He's not with you?"

"No, the idiot ran down the side of the mountain."

"Oh shit."

We skidded down the side of the hill with the rest of our squad, looking for what I presumed was a man with a hole in his chest and blood-soaked clothing. I hadn't even thought of Foley being shot when I had been glaring down the scope.

No fire came from the distance and we all relaxed for one second mentally, as one of two obstacles was overcome. We finally came near the bottom next to some rocks that were laying on top of one another. In the bushes next to it was a man lying on his side with the biggest white-toothed grin you'd ever seen, and the dirtiest face in the platoon.

"Nice shooting Granger, maybe that should be your rifle."

"Fuck you, Foley, I'm more of a semi-auto man. But I think I got four with three shots."

"REALLY? Son of a bitch. Once that guy fired, I hit the deck hard. Hit about ten feet in front of me. I knew he wasn't going to shoot again though. I saw the other two fuckers go down in the left and right bunkers. Clean hits."

Mayfield pulled him up. "We couldn't get a bead on those fuckers with our mortars. Kept hitting short and then way the fuck behind them. Not to mention we were pinned down like a bunch of beached whales. We finally got our wits about us and were able to do some sharpshooting of our own. Now it's nice and quiet for once!"

"Good," I replied. I then noticed the red garment wrapped around my ankle. The pain was starting to present itself now. Adrenaline had kicked that wound out of my mind the whole time we were looking for Foley.

Mayfield noticed me looking at it. "You gonna be mobile?"

"Yeah, I'll be okay."

"All right men. We're gonna camp, but be on extra careful watch tonight."

"What's the damage?" I didn't want to really know, but we needed to keep track of numbers.

"Lost about seven. Two were wounded also. Not the worst I guess."

"Yeah. Now we're at what…forty-seven with Daviss gone?"

"Yep. Enjoy your evening boys."

That's a fuck of a way to end a conversation like that. What a bipolar fuck Mayfield is turning out to be.

Most of the men started clearing out areas to lay for a while. A little bit of murmuring and some conversation started up. Foley jabbed me as I threw my pack on the ground.

"I know you didn't get two with one bullet, Granger."

"How the fuck do you know that?"

"I shot the fucker as he fired at me with your piece of shit semi-auto. Saw him go down right next to the gunner you took out. But the guys don't need to know that."

Foley took his pack and put it under his head for the sleep he desperately needed.

This fucker is the best shot, isn't he?

I lay on my back and closed my eyes. I looked over when I heard rustling coming from a pack next to me. Foley took out a piece of *Pink Bison*, winked at me, and went back to get some rest. I treated myself to a piece as well. I finally started to entertain the dark plane in front of my face when Foley leaned over and poked me. *Man, this dude is all hyped up about something.*

"What's up?" I whispered.

Foley handed me a small black and white photo that showed a man and woman. The man was dressed in short boots with creased pants and a collared shirt. The woman wore a subtle dress, but was one of the most beautiful I had ever seen.

"Those are my parents. They gave me the most wonderful childhood. My dad made me work hard, but always made time for fun and educated me on how to keep up the farm back home. He was a blacksmith and my mom was a homemaker. Her pie was the best in town."

I noticed tears running down the sides of Foley's face as he continued to speak. "I thought about them right before I ran down the side of that hill. I thought I was going to die. If something happens to me, please carry this photo and this picture of Lucy with you. They'll bring you good fortune."

I smiled back at him with a nod. He then took the photo and placed it back in his helmet. He wiped the drops from his eyes and slowly rolled over to face away from me. I took my own picture of my parents out of my helmet and stared at it for the longest time. After a bit, I toned down my whimpering as I cried myself to sleep.

Chapter 11

I swear we hadn't walked this much since basic. I'm guessing it was about five hours straight, up narrow trails that wound through overgrown brush and gradually inclined up the rest of the canyons. It was testing our limits, even though we'd been through hell for how many weeks now…

We were all confused as to why we hadn't met any resistance. It was mostly hillside we were climbing, so Mayfield's theory was that it was too risky to put a bunch of fuckers on the ridges. Mayfield looked rough. You'd swear he'd aged twenty years in just a few days. But everyone looked like shit. Tired and clueless, we continued our trek until dark. We camped on a slope. Three watch groups: two on each end and then one in the middle. It was like a long train of dumb fucks lined up sleeping head-to-toe. *Well, at least if we get shot, we get a nice fifty-foot joyride down to the treetops below.*

Foley and I were on watch at opposite ends. We were not even a quarter-mile apart. I had my semi-auto while Foley decided to take his submachine gun out for the event. This was surprising. Nobody ever saw him take that thing out. Gus was in the middle, sitting on his backpack with a rifle like mine laying across his lap. He had a banana in one hand and a small book in the other. *Kinda looks like a miniature bible…* All of the other soldiers, all forty-some of us that were left, including us three, were laying in between us. Some were sleeping, some were twiddling dog tags in their hands, and some were looking straight up at the sky without blinking an eye. We had been on watch for about two and a half hours. Long time to hear absolutely nothing. Ironically, Mayfield and Haywood had landed themselves at the foot of Foley and I. Haywood had been awake the whole time, one-handing his machine gun.

"Think we should prop the thirties?" he said to me, finally, breaking the silence.

"Nah, there ain't shit out here," I replied. I felt like as each day passed, I cared less about what the fuck went on. "…we all gotta die sometime," I muttered underneath my breath.

Haywood gave me an odd look and shook his head. He was still trying to pry something positive out of me. "What are you gonna do for a living when you get back home?"

I chuckled at this one. *Alright, he's making an effort…*

"Honestly? I'd like to own a hardware store. Work at that while selling shit on the side, fix up crap laying around, and give people good deals instead of raping them in the ass like the big ones do…how about you Stanley?"

A big smile came across his face after I dropped the first name on him. "Well, I want to be a mechanic of some sort. Maybe heavy-duty machinery. Maybe aircraft. I like that shit."

"Why didn't you go into that when you signed up for the military?"

Haywood looked in the distance for a long while before answering. "I thought I wouldn't be doing my duty if I just settled for a non-battle position. I have the courage to lead these men and I knew it would be hell. But once I got home, I knew that I could relax and say I did the most I could for this country. Now if they would only bump me up in rank…"

I stared at Stanley for a long time, slightly nodding my head up and down, thinking of something encouraging to reply with. Finally, I spat something out. "You're doing a hell of a job man."

SHOOP. My whole body went numb. The sound had sent the worst chill down my spine that I had experienced up to this point. I stared for what felt like forever at the hole in the middle of the forehead of Haywood. A small line of blood bolted straight down the middle of his face as I instinctively jumped on top of him.

"TAKE COVER! DOWN ON THE SIDE OF THE HILL! LET'S MOVE!" Mayfield was shouting orders to the rest of the groggy-eyed men who jolted out of a deep sleep and proceeded to slide on their asses down the side of the ridge. The medic had come rushing over and kicked my bag down the hill as he yelled "GO!" to me. I whipped my head back around one more time as I scurried away to see the pale expression that left Haywood dead on the trail. *It was that fucking sniper again…*

After a few minutes, everyone calmed down and Foley came crawling over to where I was. Stuck behind a thick tree on a steep slope, there wasn't much room for two people to hide. But Foley made himself comfortable as he sat adjacent to me, him being closer to the trail above.

"That fucker is still out there!" he shouted as a whisper to me.

"I know, he got Haywood," I replied. Foley stared at me for a second, looked up at the trail, and then back at me.

"Son of a bitch. I saw the flash too. Fucker is probably gone though."

"He had to have been higher than us. Can't see us from below. And he only shot once, so he must have been in some sort of clearing."

Foley scanned to the west while everyone else continued to look around like a bunch of dumbasses. "There."

He pointed to a small clearing in the trees where some large trunks all circled around. You could see huge branches that were definitely large enough to sustain the weight of a man.

"It's high, it's in the cover, but it's still accessible for firing. I'll signal to Mayfield and keep an eye through the scope for a while. You watch my six Granger."

"Copy that, don't miss the bastard." I had been on watch for hours already, but so had Foley. I had no excuse not to stay awake. Plus the adrenaline was pumping, so that helped things. Mayfield signaled back to us and he got a few guys from fifteenth to also keep an eye on the surrounding area of the new target.

"You ready?!" I awoke as I felt a poke in my ribs from Foley's elbow. "Wake the fuck up, I got him back up there."

"… Yeah man, I got your back," I was lying. I had fallen asleep. I looked at the sky. *Sun coming up and peaking over the trees… dawn… must have been out for three hours…*

I glanced around at the men from fifteenth, sixtieth, and sixty-second. Everyone was alert but tired. Nobody close to Mayfield dared to even blink an eye as they all stared so elegantly toward the treetops in the distance-

BANG. The noise rang through my ears as I looked through my binoculars toward the trees. Slung over a branch was a man missing part of his shoulder. His gun fell to the ground as a feeling of relief swept throughout the crew.

"Tango down," Mayfield said with a smile. "You got him, Foley."

Foley took his head away from the scope of his rifle. "That sucked."

"Yeah man, all good now," I reassured.

"Let's get back on that trail and keep moving boys." Mayfield was nearly running back up the hill.

"Now Daviss and Haywood can both thank you," Gus toted to Foley as he ran up next to us.

Foley frowned and gave a nod as he continued up the path next to me. He took out a piece of *Pink Bison*, gave half to Gus, and put the rest in his mouth. I took out a piece myself as well, patted Foley on the shoulder, and continued up the ridge to the trail.

"I have no idea where this trail leads," said Gus. "But I can tell you it's nowhere good."

"Fuck you, Gus," I replied. I got a smile out of Foley.

"He ain't wrong," Foley remarked as we reached the path.

"Alright, men," Mayfield chimed out. "We are now going to walk about half a mile to where the trail quits winding. From what dispatch told me, there's resistance at the path that cuts across the top of the canyons. If we can get past them, fortieth is on the other side with support and about three hundred men waiting. Trouble is, they can't hit the fuckers from the rear. So, we are at it alone again. But this is it, boys, if we can make this, perhaps we can relax for a while."

Everyone grinned at this, but only momentarily as we realized that we were probably outnumbered once again.

"He wasn't wrong," Foley said as I felt a slap on the back from him. Following him up the trail, I looked behind me where Gus was taking a piss to bring up the rear.

"Gus, quit jerking off and save your energy for the top of the canyons," I joked.

"Hey, I wanted to touch my dick one more time before I might lose it, Elliott."

"Well, better you than some poor lady."

"It'd be their privilege."

"Faggot." I smiled at Gus as he joined up with Foley and I for the trip to Armageddon.

Chapter 12

The treacherous trek led us to the point where we could look down about two hundred feet. This is why this was labeled as the "canyons." You could see cliffs in the distance that sprayed from our central point. They rose nearly adjacent to the horizon and served as tabletops for the sun to shed its heat upon. Still, the trees provided a nice ceiling for us from that awful sun. It was about a hundred out there, but everyone's spirits were lifted by the scenery. We were walking down a man-made path about 30 feet wide. Kinda stupid to be doing so. It was obviously where the enemy had once traveled before us and would be the conspicuous path for us to continue on. Maybe that's why Mayfield had led us down it. *Can't question his judgment now…a little too late for that shit…*

A hand went up at the front of our line. Everyone stopped and looked around cautiously. There were birds making stupid noises that more than likely alerted the enemy we were near.

"Mortar team! You sit at the outside flanks! Granger and Gus on the thirties! Foley, you'll be with me next to the rest of our guys! Everyone else buckle down with your weapon at the ready!" Mayfield had ordered us to camp behind the last of the thick group of trees that we knew existed. Up ahead were clear woods followed by a small pond and brush that was full of what I assumed were poisonous flowers and botany. It was apparent that there had been recent activity in that stretch, so I was happy that Mayfield had spotted it right away.

We had some logs to set the thirties on and everyone started to dig fox holes. I started feeding the belt clip into the machine gun when Foley started to talk to me as he dug our hole.

"So where are we on the watch schedule? I think I'm way the fuck ahead since you decided to sleep last night." He was smiling at me as I knew he had me beat.

"Do I owe you an entire night now?" I replied sarcastically.

"No, but you get first watch tonight and you owe me more gum. I'm out."

I dug in my pack quickly and grabbed the last pack of *Pink Bison* that I had. "Make it last sir."

"Oh dude, I'm not gonna take your last one, I was just playin'."

"Nah, it's okay. I have a good amount left in mine. Plus, mine's got the exclusive cartoon that only a few packs had on the back!" I had a large grin as I bragged to Foley.

"Looks like this foxhole is only gonna fit one guy after that comment." Foley laughed as we went about our business. *Foley has really opened up these past couple weeks. Glad to see him not being so damn short all the time.*

Nobody had noticed any activity since we had camped earlier that day. Dispatch didn't really know if the enemy was near or had left the area, so Mayfield was in a rough mood. But everyone was in decent spirits. The thirty-nine of us were reassured. Even though the last thing we may see was each other, we were all okay with that. The pride set in for a little while as we realized the country that we were defending was protected and our loved ones were safe. I'd even say that morale was at a fricken all-time high. Son of a bitch.

*****

The flak had gradually come about in the afternoon. Mortars, slings of machine gun rounds, even some Gatling gun-like shit that nobody could figure out. We all lay prone behind the downed trees and incomplete banks we had made earlier that day. I had my hand glued to the trigger of the thirty cal. as a man from sixtieth kept my belt clip full. The bullets passed through his hands in slow motion, as I'd rather watch him than my fucking head getting blown off.

"MORTARS! PUT SOME FUCKING ROUNDS ON THEM BASTARDS!" Mayfield was shouting orders that barely made it into the ears of the teams on each end. Gus was shooting more conservatively than I was, as occasionally, you'd see him mouth a *fuck yeah* when he knew blood was shed across the pond.

"GRANGER! YOU'RE OUT MAN!" The man from sixtieth looked at me as if I'd lost a lung or something.

"FUCK!" I grabbed my semi-auto simultaneously to him doing so as we took a spot behind the banks and started to look for targets. I had no idea where the fuck Foley was. Hadn't seen him in a couple of hours.

"GRENADES!" Mayfield roared as we all saw rock-like figures hopping down the woods toward us. We all ducked as more deafening blasts ignited around us. I could hear the shouts of men getting hit by the shrapnel and the occasional thud of a fucker near us getting taken out. I continued to fire in the distance ahead. I noticed that shadowy figures came across the pond now, guns with silver blades on the ends pointing right at us. *Holy shit!* As I prepared to fire another thirty rounds into the two fuckers that pursued, they both dropped in my sights about a second apart. I then looked to the left where more were trying to nail our foxholes. Two more down. *Foley!*

A thwarted plan led the enemy to stop sending men over the pond and further down the road right at us. This bought me a few seconds to look behind me. At about my seven o'clock, I saw a figure about twenty-five feet up in the woods with a glistening bolt-action rifle and a man looking down the scope firing away. Foley was kneeling on a large branch and was shooting and reloading constantly. I smiled as I turned back to the battlefield. However, we weren't gaining anything and men were starting to drop like flies. Mayfield had radioed in for air support. A desperate attempt to stop the madness wasn't going to do shit for us.

We fought for hours as more of our men were lost and ammo was decreasing significantly. At about eight o'clock is when I grabbed my last clip and shoved it in my rifle. Thirties were gone. Mortars had about two fucking loads left and everyone was resorting to holding onto their pistols for when the men came back into our foxholes. Foley had come down from the tree furiously once the mortars had started to pinpoint his location. We were hunkered down hard but knew that we had to go down with a fight. I mean, there was no fucking way we'd get out of this one.

As I looked down my sights, I saw some movement in the bushes that were about seventy yards away. I decided to shoot in that general direction.

BAM! A monster explosion erupted in the distance when it appeared that I had hit the fuel tank or oil can of something or another. A fire started to sweep left and firing in the distance halted momentarily.

Now I was full of adrenaline and scared as shit. I instinctively fixed my bayonet. I knew what was coming, as did Foley, as did Gus… as did everyone. Earlier, Mayfield had told us that push comes to shove, we go kamikaze on their ass and guerrilla our way to victory or death. It was obvious they thought we had nothing left and that we'd hunker down before doing something as stupid as we were about to. I thought I'd be dead long before this would happen, so I hadn't comprehended it until now. *Too late.*

"NOW! NOW! NOW!" screeched Mayfield as we all sprung over the banks and out of our foxholes and began sprinting through the opening ahead. I had my rifle out in front of me as I looked around at the green leaves that had water droplets on them near the pond. Oh, how time stood still for that moment. Oh, how I remember that Monica wore that short dress that one night and how Hal had cried when I left and how Haywood had died in front of my face the night before. These thoughts circled my head as I felt that I was watching myself run through the woods toward whatever lay behind those bushes. I couldn't feel my legs as they trudged through the terrain and triumphed through the water. *Thirty yards left.* There was loud shouting as everyone prepared for their death and for whatever may come before such. *Twenty yards.* The adrenaline was fierce as I started to angle up my weapon for the motherfucker sitting in a trench that deserved to die. *Ten yards.* I now yelled myself. No! I ROARED as I jumped up on the sloped bank and came through the opening of leaves next to my comrades who were alongside me the whole way…

I let my blade slash through the first inkling of a human body figure before me and pulled it out just as quickly as blood sprayed on my cheek and camouflaged the face of the man in front of me. I looked up to find another man behind him and ducked as he swung his weapon at my head. His guts turned into a scarlet, tomato-like color as I turned back around into him and sliced his abdomen wide open. I was in a daze. I was MAD. I was ON POINT. I was UNSTOPPABLE. I looked to the left and right as I saw some of my brothers fall to their death while others sprung to victory with each swing of their weapon. I turned back to find two coming at me with their own blades as I ducked, sending one's momentum over my head, falling into the trench behind me, and proceeded to trip the man in front of me. Whipping my body around, I stabbed into the skull of the man on the ground next to me and fired at the individual struggling to get out of the trench. Two more down. Things were starting to clear ahead. In fact, it almost looked as if the figures were running away from us. It didn't matter. I continued to chase them for twenty more yards when I felt my head hit the ground with a massive THUD. I looked up, ready to glare into the eyes of the man who was going to put a knife through my throat. Trembling, my body forced itself to relax when I heard the deafened sound of "Granger" come from the mouth of the figure on top of me.

I snapped out of my trance. I looked up and saw Foley on top of me with his rifle laying horizontally across my chest. He was breathing hard and had the worst, the most scared look that I had seen on him ever.

"GRANGER. THEY'RE RETREATING. FORTIETH WILL TAKE CARE OF THE REST. DIDN'T YOU HEAR MAYFIELD YELL OUT TO STAND DOWN?" Foley wasn't really yelling, but more so lecturing me.

I lay silent for a while before answering. "No…sorry…shouldn't we be on alert again?" I was still in a daze.

"NO, GRANGER. IT'S OVER. WE TOOK 'EM."

Foley got off me and helped me to my feet slowly. Gus and Mayfield came running over all fired up.

"HELL OF A SHOW, GRANGER!" Mayfield sarcastically exclaimed. "When we came over the bank, it was obvious that we outnumbered them. I was shocked to see you take out four men like that when we had the firepower to do so already. Why didn't you stand down like I ordered after we made it across the pond and onto the bank?"

"Never heard ya," I sheepishly replied. "Doesn't matter, there were other men doing what I was, so nobody heard ya."

"Granger," Foley calmly said as he put a hand on my shoulder. "Everyone else was on the bank firing off one knee. There were only about twenty guys, aside from the five that were burning in the foxholes to the south."

"NO! I saw them! There were men dying and taking blows to the head and killing these bastards—"

"ENOUGH!" Mayfield yelled loudly, probably the loudest I had ever heard him yell actually. "Granger! You were the only one who was using your bayonet on those worthless fucks. You were the only one who took out four of them by firing one round and stabbing three of them. Granger, you were in a trance. Nothing around you was real. Only what was in front of you was."

I stared at Mayfield. I was astonished, embarrassed, and displeased with my performance. I acted stupidly while everyone else was following orders. I could have gotten more people killed when they were RETREATING. *What the fuck is the matter with me man?*

Foley knew it was time to let me cool off and changed the subject. "How many left?"

"Took a headcount," sighed Mayfield. Fifteenth has seven, we have four, sixtieth has nine, and sixty-second has three.

Foley did the math instantly. "Twenty-three men? And it's me, you, Granger, and Gus from our squad?!"

"Yeah. Not my goal. But that's reality."

"Fuck."

We were walking through the woods again, but not on alert. We had pushed the enemy back toward fortieth where they made the mistake of not standing down. Earlier that morning, we had been told that fortieth had eliminated the last of the threat. *Good, don't let one more of those fuckers live.* Now, our only goal was a one-mile walk to camp where our status remained at-large. Foley and I walked quietly the whole way. I had lost my last pack of gum during the altercation from last night. Foley was kind enough to split his with me. I popped another piece in. Last night, I had taken my helmet off and stared at the picture of my parents. I thought a lot about them and Monica. And Foley too. And Lucy for a while. I smiled as I recalled myself sleeping peacefully that night, holding the photos in my hand. I also had slipped Haywood's picture of the slutty broad in my helmet. Maybe that's why I had lived. It's as if the monstrous, fuck-it-let's-do-it attitude had been inherited by me from him. And that was all right. We were safe for the time being.

Chapter 13

We had reached the camp and all took a night to recover. The next morning, guys from fortieth were out and about, counting dog tags, telling stories, and laughing as we awaited to hear if we all were going home or not. Our platoon had joined in the fun and were starting to actually feel comfortable for once. Foley had the picture of Lucy in his hand as he was talking to a few other guys when Mayfield spoke up.

"Listen up! Sources have told me that our own Allan Foley has reached a few milestones worthy of recognition. Foley! Come up here please!"

Foley walked up there as whistling and joking remarks were made during his trudge that brought him next to Mayfield.

"Foley," continued Mayfield. "With your triumphant efforts and remarkable sharpshooting in the canyons, dispatch and I have confirmed that you not only reached your one-hundredth confirmed kill, but that you have also eliminated the sniper whom took over two-hundred people's lives in combat in his lifetime. Well done sir. Your comrades and country thank you!"

Roars and shouts of encouragement echoed throughout the camp as Foley only slightly grinned. When the chanting of "FOLEY! FOLEY!" began, Allan got their attention and hushed them momentarily.

After a long pause of not knowing what to say, he threw in a piece of gum, lit a cigarette, and remarked, "Couldn't have done it without my man Granger," as he pointed at me in the crowd.

I nodded in return to Foley while Gus gave me a thumbs up.

"All right men, the news you've wanted. Most resistance has been accounted for in our region. The canyons were our goal and we reached it valiantly. You will all be shipped back home in four days."

Now EVERYONE yelled and began hugging one another. Tears filled the eyes of myself and Foley as he rushed toward me and gave me a hug.

"We made it man," Foley coughed out as our hug finished.

"Yessir. Now we can have peace again," I replied.

Foley went over by our tent and grabbed his rifle. He picked it up and looked at it astonishingly, as if he'd never seen anything like it before.

I walked over next to him. "I'm sure they'll let you keep that."

Foley looked at me despairingly. He then pressed the release on the bottom of the rifle next to the trigger guard and pulled the bolt out of it. The *A.F.* shined wonderfully in the sunlight.

"Nah man," he finally said holding up the bolt. "I'll keep this as my trophy, but this rifle has killed too many people for me to ever look at it again."

I hesitated for a second. He was right. A hundred people is a lot of life to be removed from Earth, no matter what the circumstance.

I finally looked at him and smiled. "You saved your parents, Lucy, my parents, and Monica man. At least look at it that way."

Foley smiled and threw his gum off to the side. "Always right, aren't you ya fucker?"

*****

The broom was starting to show its age now. The bristles were scattered and the wood had worn down on the spots where one would place his/her hands. Still, I swept away as the day was nearing the end. Another long one. Lots of people had come in for paint, as summer had reared its ugly head again.

I walked over to the cash register. I looked at the side of the tray that faced me. *Property of Granger Hardware.* Man, it still had a nice ring to it. Every time I looked at that thing, I thought of Haywood. It was sad that my dreams were realized while his had been shattered in a matter of seconds. I kept the picture of that girl underneath the tray and looked at it occasionally. *Man, what a babe.*

It had been about a year since I had left the military. My parents resided in the same small town in Indiana that I did. It was good to see them on a daily basis after not seeing them for nearly a year previously. I had taken what money

I had when I got back and bought Hal's store from him. He was so thrilled to see me return and was even more happy to finally retire. I had furnished the joint with more counters and pegboard to fulfill my dream of making it into a more defined hardware store. I never came to work with a bad attitude and loved what I did. It was satisfying knowing that the American Dream was still alive, even after one goes through hell.

The clock read 5:58 as I looked out the window at the figure whom walked with a huge grin on her face. I smiled instantly.

"Hi, honey," Monica said as she came through the door in her sundress and heels. *I swear them dresses will never get any longer…God, I love it…*

"Hi, Ms. Fiancée," I joked as I gave her a kiss. We were planning on getting married in the fall and were going to move into a bigger house down the road in a few weeks. Life was good. Nah. Life was fucking fantastic.

"Hey, a message came for you today." She handed me a slip of paper as I opened to read it. "I gotta go get food, but I'll see you at home. Love you!"

"Love ya, too," I replied, still staring at the note. I opened it to find a date of *May 3rd* at the top followed by chicken scratch that read:

Dear Granger, my right-hand man. Hope you been well! Just writing to stay in touch. Lucy and I are married now and are awaiting our son Leroy to enter the world. We named him after Daviss and are so happy living here in Iowa. I hope that you aren't being an asshole to Monica, but then again, you are an asshole always (ha-ha).

Anyways, I heard that you are a self-employed man now. Congrats! I am working for a sheet metal company and am making a great living. Rumor has it that Gus is a teacher now…poor students.

Anyways, please write back if you're able to man. Miss ya and maybe our paths will cross again.

FOLEY
P.S. I kept one piece of gum to remind me of ya.

I grabbed the very last piece of an unopened *Pink Bison* stick of gum from my pocket and brought it up to my face. *Me too, man. Me too.*